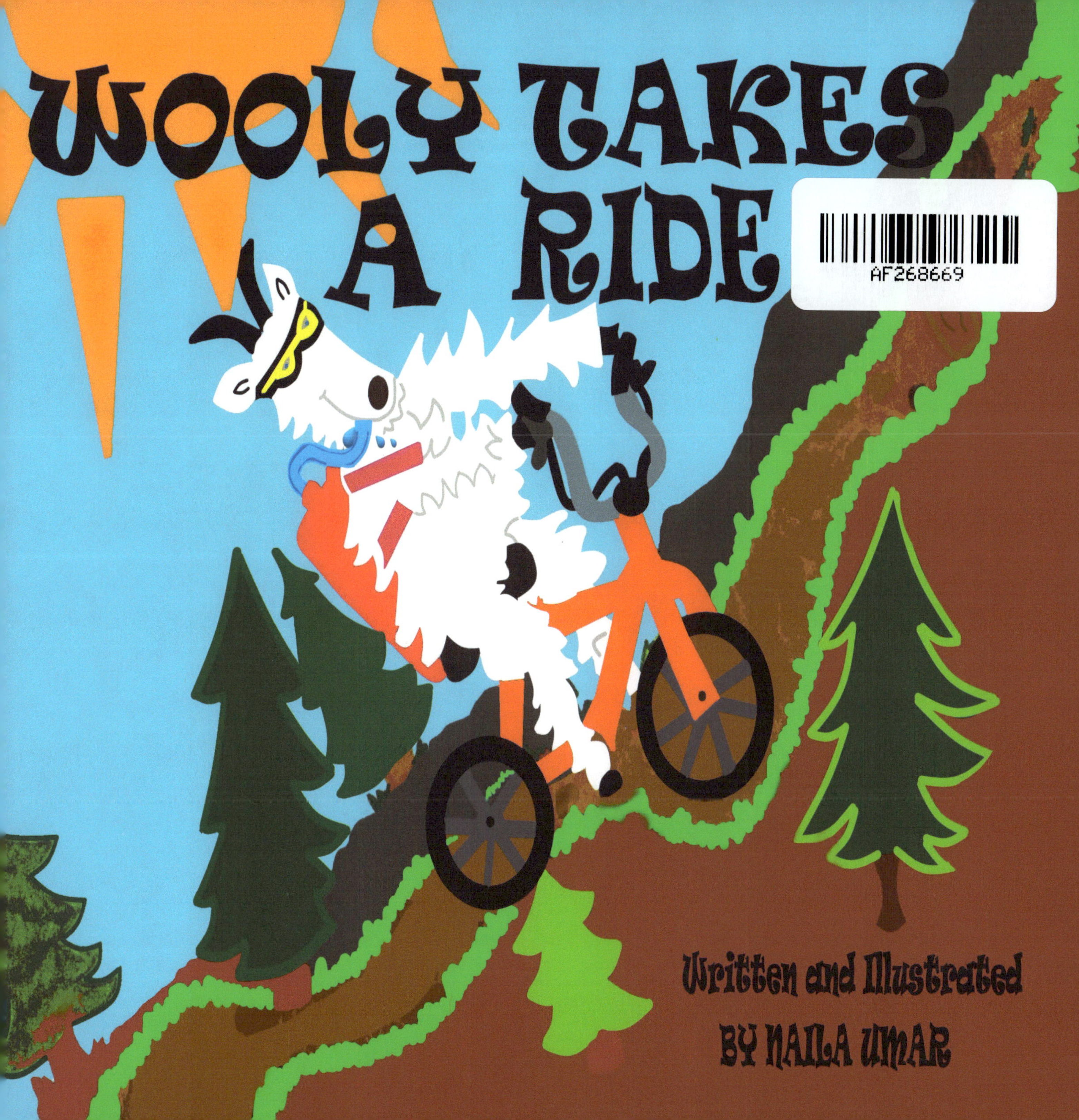

WOOLY TAKES A RIDE
AF268669
Written and Illustrated
BY NAILA UMAR

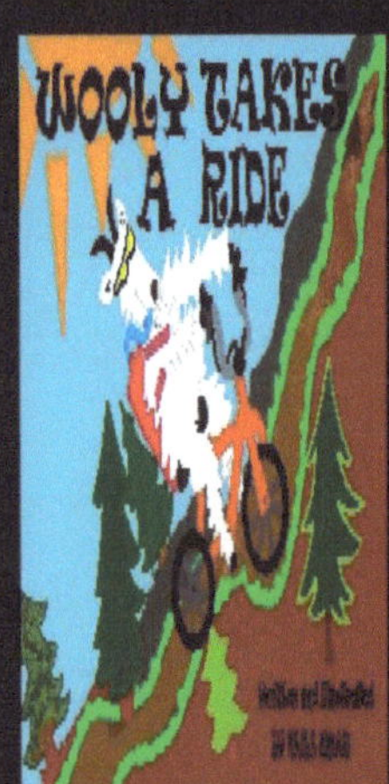

Wooly Takes A Ride

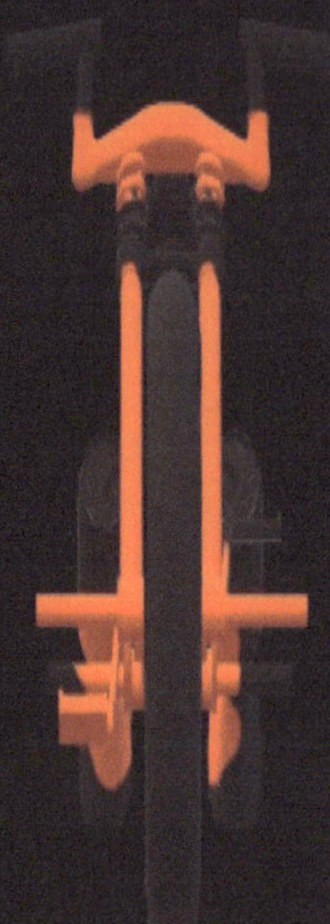

Story made in Canada

KidsBooksByNaila LLC

Library of Congress 2022

ISBN 978-1-77 5173-2-8

This book is dedicated to all the little groms and gromettes that have a passion for anything! Don't give your passions up. You can do ANYTHING. Also, shout out to the love of my life, my son Xavier (bubs), nephews Jaden and Jory and my late brother Javed who always did something rad!

Clear across the forest where the cliffs run so steep, lived a mountain goat named Wooly who really loved to leap.

He would leap and he would run on the rocky dirt trails, and he would graze on the gravel while waving his tail.

One day Wooly got bored on the hill and he sat there in thought as he stared at the mill. As he watched all the mountains that stood proud around him, he spotted a boy, with a bike, on the rim.

Now that looks like fun!!!!!
Wooly thought to himself, "now that looks like fun, I want a bike now to ride in the sun"!

Wooly ran and ran until he caught up to the boy. " I would like very much if you would lend me your toy". The boy looked at Wooly and said with a frown, " the bike will take you in places around, though this you should know as well my good friend, you must look at bikes as you would look at tools, there are a big list of bicycle rules!

It is not a toy that is only for play, you must be very careful as you ride it I say! Now Wooly was a little impatient you see, he just wanted to pedal and then shout out with glee. He hopped on his seat and put his hands on the bars, he pedaled and pedaled and rode as fast as a car!

The dirt path was all narrow all covered in leaves and the trees crowded over as he started to weave!

Wooly was having trouble going up the big mountain and all he could think of was a big water fountain. At first the mountain was going downhill then up it started climbing taking all of his will!

Wooly pedaled and pedaled until he could no longer soar, he must have climbed at least five miles or more! His hooves kept on slipping off the pedals you see as he did not have the right shoes that would fit you or me. The shoes help you stick your feet to the pedals so that you can ride really fast in the race and win medals!

He caught his breath at the top of the climb and noticed how late it had gotten in time. The sun was going down and it was getting dark in the sky. He could not believe he was up there so high!

After hours of riding up the long skinny path, he had gotten all dirty and felt he needed a bath; It was not over for Wooly quite yet, now he had to go down and quite fast you can bet.

He climbed back on the bike for the fun to begin, if he had been racing the bike he was sure he would win! He started going down on that dirt covered trail, Wooly felt great as he started to sail! Then all of a sudden he remembered the boy, who said "be wise don't treat the bike as a toy". He did not know why the boy was so worried, it was so much fun as down the hill he did hurry!

The wind was blowing all through his thick furry coat, he was having a blast, that brave little goat!
Then all of a sudden as he looked at the ground, he saw something coming that looked kind of round...

There up ahead lay a biggen wooden log, this was not quite like when he went out for a jog!!

He could not just jump over this thing in his way, so he lifted his hooves off the pedals and stretched, Wooly closed his sweet eyes as he started to sway. As the bike went across the log that lay still, he remembered the boy from earlier that day. He now knew why the boy had told him those things but all Wooly could do now, was wish he had WINGS!!!

His body went flying off the bike oh so high. In the distance was Woolys voice starting to cry.

He landed his body on a pile of
leaves, it could have been
worse had he landed in trees.
He got up from the track and
shook off the dirt, and then he
made sure that he didn't get
hurt. He had a few scratches
and some scrapes here and
there. In his blue shorts he
noticed a tear.
It wasn't so bad for
Wooly that time but next
time he knew that he
would come prepared.

He would bring a helmet to wear on the ride and with pads, his knees and elbows he would hide. He wished he had listened to the boy on that day and not gone so fast on his own little way.

Maybe next time Wooly
will know what to do,
he will listen to others
who have ridden bikes
too! Wooly says, "wear
your safety gear when
riding your bikes and
even when the young
ones are riding their
trikes!"

Kids Books By Naila

Coming soon! More Stories to engage your adventurous spirit!

OUT NOW!!   OUT NOW!!

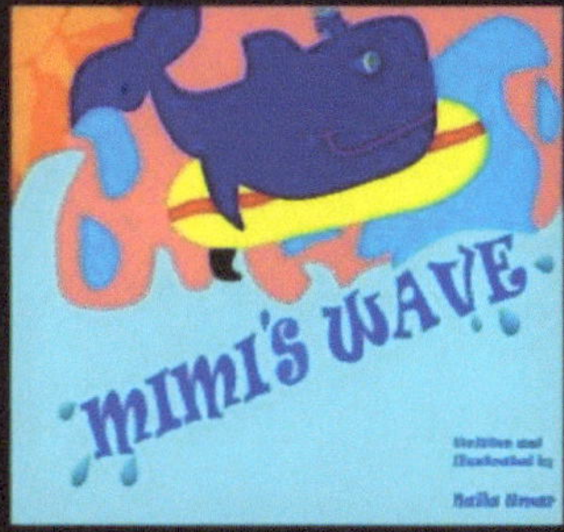

Available on Amazon now!!

Available on paperback now
at www.kidsbooksbynaila.com
and www.kidsbooksbynaila.ca

More Stories To Come

* Sammy Spiders Rock Wall

* Polly's Mom

* Ali's Journey

* Archie's True Wish

* The Rooster Alarm

* Eileen's Home

BENEFITS OF SPORTS ON KIDDOS!

1. BETTER EYES!
2. HEALTHY WEIGHT
3. MOTOR SKILLS
4. SOCIAL SKILLS
5. SELF CONFIDENCE
6. SPORTSMANSHIP
7. FUN!!
8. STRONG HEART
9. STRONG LUNGS
10. STRONG BONES

SPORTS ARE AWESOME

www.ingramcontent.com/pod-product-compliance
Lightning Source LLC
Chambersburg PA
CBHW042143030726
47599CB00002B/598